ISBN 1 85854 721 0
Published by Brimax Books Ltd, Newmarket,
England, CB8 7AU, 1998.
Second printing 1998.
Printed in Spain.

A Puppy With a Waggly Tail

By Gill Davies

Illustrated by Sally Hynard

A puppy with a waggly tail
Has come to live with us.
He is so soft and cuddly
And he likes a lot of fuss.

We have given him some toys –
A rubber ring, a bone, a ball.
But it is my mother's slipper
That he likes the best of all.

He doesn't like it on his own.

He cries and sounds so sad at night.

So I sneak down to see him

And he wiggles with delight.

He jumps up on my lap
And tries to lick my nose.
Then he runs around in circles
And barks and pounces on my toes.

When I have to go upstairs

He looks with big, sad eyes.

I tell him to be quiet.

I feel sad to hear his cries.

Sometimes he leaves little puddles
And looks as guilty as can be.
Mother says, "He's just a baby.
He'll soon learn – you'll see."

We don't know what to call him.
Father has suggested 'Joe'.
I called him 'Wiggles' yesterday.
It's a name he seemed to know.

I love our brand new puppy
So much I think I'll burst.
And if you ask who my best friend is
He is definitely first.